Number Rhymes

to say and play!

Opal Dunn
Illustrated by Adriano Gon

FRANCES LINCOLN CHILDREN'S BOOKS

Contents

To Michael and Lily, who love numbers – O.D.

To Lisa and Emily – A.G.

Several of the rhymes have been written by the author to make understanding of numbers easier for young children.
Any rhyme that is not traditional is derived from its use in nursery and infant schools with native speaker
or first foreign language learners whom the author has taught in her long career.
If there is copyright for any of these rhymes, it is an oversight and the author and publishers
will be pleased to acknowledge it in future editions.

Number Rhymes to Say and Play! copyright © Frances Lincoln Limited 2003
Compilation copyright © Opal Dunn 2003
Illustrations copyright © Adriano Gon 2003

The right of Opal Dunn to be identified as the author of this work
has been asserted by her in accordance with
the Copyright, Designs and Patents Act, 1988.

First published in Great Britain in 2003 by
Frances Lincoln Limited, 4 Torriano Mews,
Torriano Avenue, London NW5 2RZ

www.franceslincoln.com

First paperback edition 2004

British Library Cataloguing in Publication Data available on request

ISBN 0-7112-2167-7

Printed in Singapore
3 5 7 9 8 6 4 2

Dear Parents, Carers and Teachers,

Numbers are all around children – in their homes and neighbourhoods. To use numbers and read them on the telephone, on the bus or out shopping, children need experience. They can succeed with numbers and build up confidence.

The rhymes in this book give children experiences from an early age and level of understanding. They start with 1 2 3, and progress to 5, 8 and 10. There are suggestions on how to play games with rhymes, as children who are physically involved with the language tend to understand it and pick it up more quickly. Start with the ideas in the book and build into them your own way of playing the games. The pictures with number words and symbols complement the rhymes, and children can join in reading the numbers out loud. There are rhymes to appeal to both boys and girls, and it is fun if you personalise these, letting children add their own names.

Rhymes to say and play are portable play experiences that need no equipment. They can be used anywhere and at any time. The more you say and play the rhymes together, the quicker they will become part of your child's daily life. Children who feel they can use numbers with confidence have a strong foundation on which to build future numeracy. Attitudes to experiences are formed early in life and if you can help your child feel 'I can do sums', your child will approach later numeracy with a positive attitude. So start now and have rhyme times together that are fun!

Opal Dunn

Me

Five little people fast asleep,
One by one, out they creep.
Five little people wide awake now,
One by one they take a bow.

1 2 3 4 5

HOW TO PLAY
Make your fingers into a fist.
Uncurl your fingers one by one.
When you have uncurled all of them,
make them 'bow' one by one.

Here are ten funny men,
See how they dance and play.
Two stand straight,
Two join hands,
The rest run away.

HOW TO PLAY
Hold up your ten fingers and wiggle them.
Make your two index fingers stand up
straight. Then join your two thumbs.
Tuck away the rest of your fingers
into your fist as they run away.

One
Two
Three
Four
Five

1 2 3 4 5 6 7 8 9 10

one　two　three　four　five　six　seven　eight　nine　ten

Ten fingers,
Ten toes,
Two eyes,
Just one nose.

Two little eyes to look around,
Two little ears to hear each sound,
One little nose to smell what's sweet,
One little mouth that likes to eat.

Outside

One cat,
Two cats,
I can see **three**.

Look for one more
And that makes **four**.
1 2 3 4

Two **big** apples
Under a tree.
One is for you
And one's for me.

Clap, clap, clap,
Clap like me.
1 2 3

Jump, jump, jump,
Jump with me.
1 2 3

In the country

Jump on the stepping stones,
One two three.
Jump on the stepping stones
After me.

Jump on the stepping stones,
One two three.
Jump on the stepping stones
Just like me.

Seven little children
Running down the lane,
Paddling in the puddles,
Splashing in the rain,
Talking to each other
About the showery day –
Seven little children
Going out to play.

Six little children
Walking down the lane...

Five little children
Skipping down the lane...

Naughty little monkeys

Five little monkeys bouncing on the bed,
One fell off and bumped his head.
Dad called the doctor,
The doctor said,
"Naughty little monkeys bouncing on the bed!"

Four little monkeys bouncing on the bed,
One fell off and bumped his head...

Three little monkeys bouncing on the bed,
One fell off and bumped his head...

HOW TO PLAY
Hold up five fingers to represent the monkeys.
Bounce these fingers on the palm of your other hand.
Hold your head to show it has been hurt
and make a face as if you are in pain.
Pretend to use a phone to ring the doctor.
Shake your forefinger angrily to the rhythm of the last line.

In the toy shop

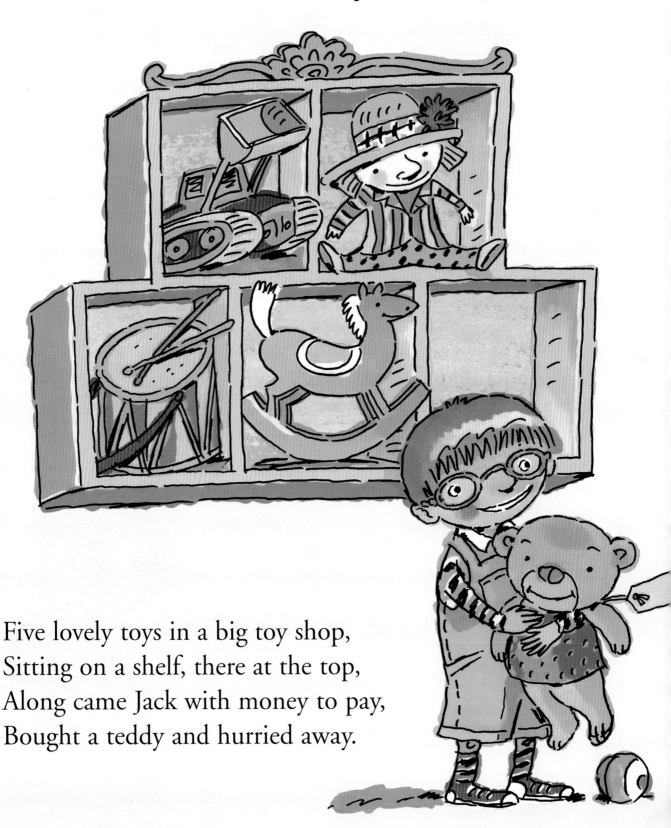

Five lovely toys in a big toy shop,
Sitting on a shelf, there at the top,
Along came Jack with money to pay,
Bought a teddy and hurried away.

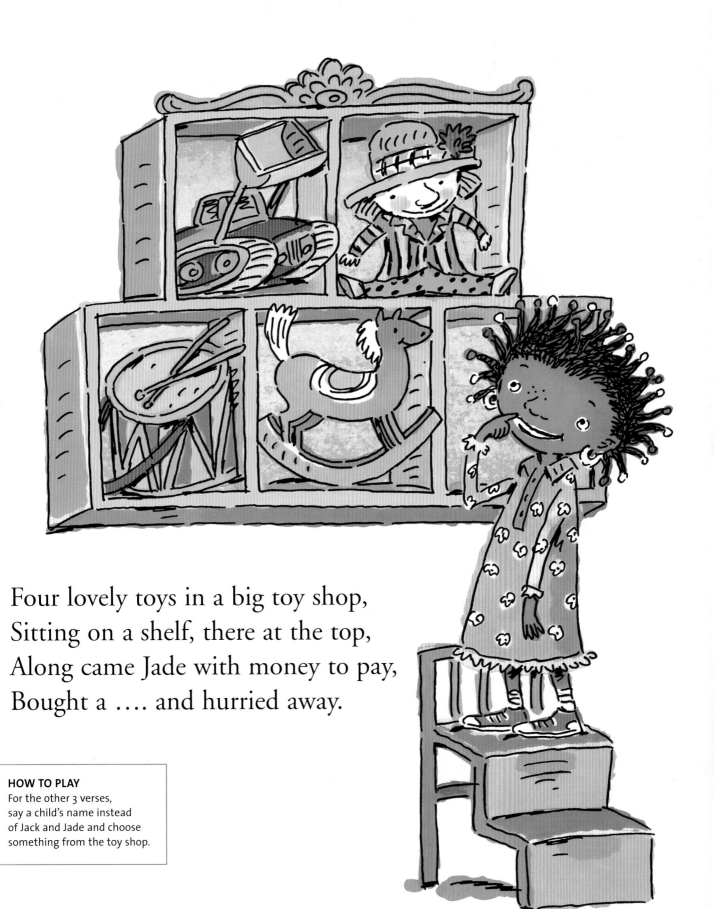

Four lovely toys in a big toy shop,
Sitting on a shelf, there at the top,
Along came Jade with money to pay,
Bought a …. and hurried away.

HOW TO PLAY
For the other 3 verses,
say a child's name instead
of Jack and Jade and choose
something from the toy shop.

In the cottage garden

1 2 3 4

Mary's at the cottage door,

5 6 7 8

Eating cherries off a plate.

> **HOW TO PLAY**
> Point to the numbers or pretend to be Mary
> and give the children a plate of pretend cherries.
> Ask "If Mary has eaten two cherries,
> how many does she have left?".

2 4 6 8

Meet me at the garden gate,
If I'm late, don't wait.

2 4 6 8

> **HOW TO PLAY**
> Hold your hands facing each other.
> As you say '2' join the tips of
> the little fingers,
> '4' join the tips of the ring fingers,
> '6' join the middle fingers
> and '8' join the index fingers.

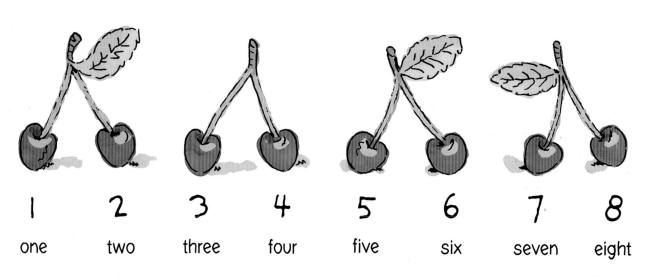

1	2	3	4	5	6	7	8
one	two	three	four	five	six	seven	eight

I can do it!

Number **1**, show your **tongue**.

Number **2**, now say **BOO!**

Number **3**, touch your **knee**.

Number **4**, point to the **door**.

Number **5**, pretend to **dive**.

Number **6**, wiggle your **hips**.

Number **7**, jump up to **heaven**.

Number **8**, stand up **straight**.

Number **9**, touch your **spine**.

Number **10**, now do it **again**.

Number One

Number Two

Number Three

Number Four

Number Five

Number Six

Number Seven

Number Eight

Number Nine

Number Ten

One little elephant

One little elephant playing in the sun,
Found it such tremendous fun
That he called for another elephant to come.

Two little elephants playing in the sun...

Ten little elephants playing in the sun,
Found it such tremendous fun.
They **didn't** call another elephant to come.

HOW TO PLAY
Make a circle holding hands.
One child is chosen to be the first elephant
and stands in the middle of the circle.
On the third line this child chooses another child
to be the second elephant. They dance around
as the children say the rhyme. On the third line
of the next verse, the second elephant
chooses a third elephant and so on until
there are ten elephants in the circle.

Ten little fir trees

Ten little fir trees
Growing in the snow.
Along comes a farmer
and cuts down one.
Oh **no no!**

Nine little fir trees
Growing in the snow.
Along comes a farmer
and cuts down one.
Oh **no no!**

Eight little fir trees...

No little fir trees
Growing in the snow.
Oh **no no!**

Ten little school children
All with a tree,
Plant them in the snow
And watch them grow!
Oh **yes yes!**

HOW TO PLAY
Hold up ten fingers with your fingertips decorated
in green to represent the fir trees standing up straight.
As a tree is cut down, fold down one finger.
Tap ten fingers on the table as you count
to ten to represent planting the new fir trees.
Then move the ten outstretched fingers
up and up to show how the trees grow.

5　　6　　7　　8　　9　　10

Off to the moon

Five little spacemen playing near the stars,
The first one said, "Let's all fly to Mars."
The second one said, "There are rockets in the air."
The third one said, "But we don't care."
The fourth one said, "Let's go up in the sky."
Then *swish* went the ship and out went the light,
And the five little spacemen flew right out of sight.

HOW TO PLAY
Hold up five fingers to represent
a spaceman and point to each in turn.
On the last line both hands join
to make a rocket that swishes away.

Zoom zoom zoom

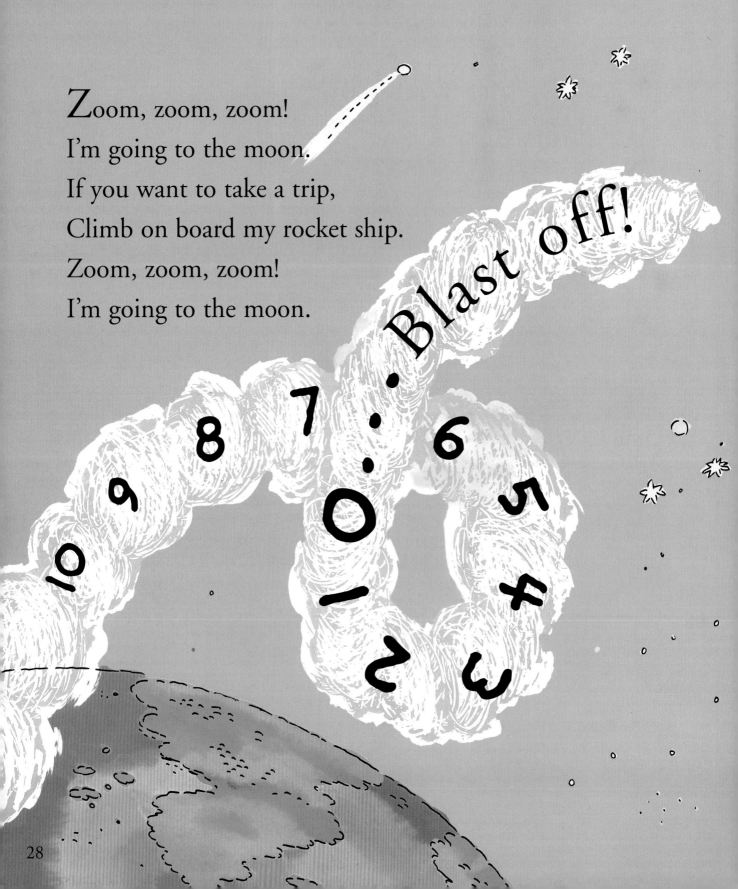

Zoom, zoom, zoom!
I'm going to the moon.
If you want to take a trip,
Climb on board my rocket ship.
Zoom, zoom, zoom!
I'm going to the moon.

Blast off!

10 9 8 7 6 5 4 3 2 1 0

Index of first lines

MORE TITLES BY OPAL DUNN IN PAPERBACK
FROM FRANCES LINCOLN

UN DEUX TROIS
First French Rhymes
Illustrated by Patrice Aggs

This first book of French rhymes takes you on an action-packed journey in French!
The book and accompanying audio cassette are filled with over 25 simple rhymes and songs.
A perfect introduction to the sounds and rhythms of another language.
Book ISBN 0-7112-0974-X
Cassette ISBN 0-7112-0975-8
Book and Cassette ISBN 0-7112-1071-3

HIPPETY-HOP, HIPPETY HAY
Growing with Rhymes from birth to age 3
Illustrated by Sally Anne Lambert

This book includes rhymes appropriate to each stage of development
from birth to age 3, and gives practical advice on how to say the rhymes
as well as actions to accompany them, games to play, and music for songs.
A really special rhyme collection for any young child.
ISBN 0-7112-1195-7

ACKER BACKA BOO!
Games to Say and Play from Around the World
Illustrated by Susan Winter

This is a collection of games from all over the world, each one accompanied
by a rhyme and clear instructions explaining how to play. With invaluable tips for parents,
teachers and carers on how to get the best out of games, this is a joyful collection
to inspire and educate children of all ages.
ISBN 0-7112-1662-2

**Frances Lincoln titles are available from all good bookshops.
You can also buy books and find out more about your favourite titles, authors and illustrators
on our website: www.franceslincoln.com**